Really Bird, Really Scared!
Text copyright © 2024 Harriet Ziefert
Illustrations copyright © 2024 Harriet Ziefert Inc.

Published in 2024 by Red Comet Press, LLC,
Brooklyn, NY

All rights reserved. No part of this book may be used or reproduced in any manner whatsoever without written permission except in the case of brief quotations embodied in critical articles and reviews.

Library of Congress Control Number: 2023941971

ISBN (HB): 978-1-63655-103-6
ISBN (EBOOK): 978-1-63655-104-3

23 24 25 26 TLF 10 9 8 7 6 5 4 3 2 1

First Edition
Manufactured in China

RedCometPress.com

Part 1:

Moon's Wish

It was the end of
a warm summer's night.

Moon was tired of shining.
She was waiting for
the first glow of sunrise.

But Sun was nowhere to be seen.

Moon made a wish:
"Please, Sun, get up!
I NEED TO GO TO BED!
I'm SO tired."

Part 2:

Really Bird's Wish

Really Bird went looking
for his friends—
Rabbit and Mouse.

He found them nearby,
huddled under a porch.

Squirrel was there—
also wondering why
it was still dark.

"If we are REALLY NICE and REALLY LOUD, maybe Sun will get up."

"Let's tell Sun to RISE and SHINE!"

"YES! Sun needs to wake up!"

I'll be ready in a jiffy — ready to shine all day long!

Ready to power up and shine on all of you!

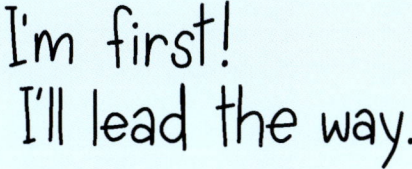

Part 3:

Sunshine

Sun sent his best golden rays
to shine on everyone.

Oh, what a beautiful day!

A beautiful day for boating!

Thank you, Sun.

Thank you for
changing the day
from scary to splendid!

"Squirrel, want to go rowing with us?"

"Okay. I don't like swimming. But I like boating."

"We both have to pull hard. At the same time!"

"Can you tell us when to stroke? It's not so easy to row a boat!"

Part 4:

Rainbow

Really Bird was right.

As suddenly as it began,
the rain stopped.

And the clouds moved on.

End of rain!
End of story?

Not quite.
Look at the sky.
A rainbow!

"Indigo is bluish purple... or purplish blue! A dark... very dark color."

"Today started out dark."

"And ended with a rainbow!"

"Without the sun, there would be no rainbows!"

"Really?"

"YES! REALLY!"

Think About/Talk About:

- Draw pictures of what you do on a sunny day.
- What do you do on a rainy day?
- How does the weather make you feel?
  Really happy?
  Really sad?
  Really scared?

- What's a protest?
  Draw some signs for something about which you would like to protest.

- What kind of weather do you wish for right now?
  Draw a picture of what you would do.

- Do you know the colors of a rainbow?
  Can you explain to a friend why there are rainbows?